Elvis the Squirrel

Written by **Tony Bradman**
Illustrated by Lizzie Finlay

A & C Black • London

First paperback edition 2007
First published 2006 by
A & C Black Publishers Ltd
38 Soho Square, London, W1D 3HB

www.acblack.com

ISBN 0-7136-7577-2
ISBN 978-0-7136-7577-1

A CIP catalogue for this book is available from the British Library.

A & C Black uses paper produced with elemental chlorine-free
pulp, harvested from managed sustained forests.

Printed and bound in Singapore by Tien Wah Press (Pte) Ltd

Chapter One

"Hurry up, Chuck!" said Elvis the Squirrel. "Breakfast is served!"

Elvis had spotted some bread on a bird table in the nearest garden and was scampering towards the fence.

His best friend Chuck was trying to keep up. "Hang on, Elvis," he said. "That food isn't meant for us. The people who live here put it out for the birds."

"So what?" said Elvis. "I don't see any birds … do you?"

"Er, no," said Chuck nervously. "In fact, it's very quiet around here this morning. A bit *too* quiet."

"Excuse me?" said Elvis. "What are you talking about now?"

"Listen, I know the bread looks tempting," said Chuck. "But we should check out the area before we rush in…" "We'll miss out if we do," said Elvis. "Come on. What could happen? Last one there's a total twit!" He jumped onto the fence and headed for the bird table.

Suddenly there was a flapping noise and a shadow fell over them. The squirrels looked up and squeaked in surprise.

A big, dark bird swooped down from the sky, grabbed Chuck in its claws and flew off, cackling with evil laughter.

"Help me, Elvis!" screamed Chuck.
But there was nothing Elvis could do.

Chapter Two

"Phew, thank goodness he's gone," somebody said.

Elvis turned and saw a group of birds landing on the bird table.

There was a slim Magpie – the one who had spoken – a plump Pigeon, a small Bluetit and a tiny Robin.

"Who was that?" said Elvis. "And where has he taken my friend?"

"*That* was Ronnie the Raven," said the Magpie. "He's terrifying."

"We keep out of the way when he's around," said the Robin.

"He's probably taken your friend to his nest," said the Bluetit.

"Where he likes to keep his victims for a while…" said the Pigeon.

"Er, I think that's enough for now," said the Robin quickly.

"…before he eats them for dinner," the Pigeon added, ignoring her.

"*WHAT*?" squeaked Elvis, horrified.
"He … he can't do that!"
"He can," said the Magpie. "Who's
going to stop him? You?"
"Yes, I *am*, actually," said Elvis.

Suddenly he felt cross with this gang
of birds. "I'll sort him out. Just tell me
where he lives, OK?"
"Listen, chum, you don't want to know,"
said the Magpie. "And why should we?
You were after *our* grub, weren't you?"

"Finders keepers," snapped Elvis.
"Now, are you going to tell me, or not?"
"Oh, go on," said the Bluetit. "Ronnie
might enjoy a dessert."

Three of the birds laughed till the tears rolled down their beaks. Only the Robin didn't join in…

Chapter Three

After a while, the Magpie told Elvis where Ronnie lived.

"What a bunch of bird-brains," the squirrel muttered as he scampered through the wood. He was sure he'd rescue his friend in no time.

At last Elvis came to Ronnie's tree.
Quietly, he climbed the one next to it
and peeped from behind its trunk.

There was Ronnie's nest … and there was Chuck! Elvis could see his friend huddled in a ball. He looked scared, but OK. Ronnie was in the nest, too, standing over Chuck, his wings folded.

Ronnie doesn't look that scary, thought
Elvis. Those silly birds have been talking
rubbish! He crouched, ready to leap into
the nest and show Ronnie who was boss.
But he brushed against a branch, and it
creaked.

CREAK

Ronnie whipped
round in a flash,
spread his wings…

...and instantly seemed

Enormous !!

A massive claw shot out and grabbed Chuck by the neck. Ronnie's wickedly sharp beak gleamed, and Chuck whimpered.

"Who's there?" Ronnie hissed, his evil eyes glinting as they scanned the nearby trees. "I'll rip you to pieces if you try to steal my dinner."

Elvis ran away as fast as his little legs could carry him.

Chapter Four

Elvis didn't stop running till he came to
a tree on the far side of the wood. He sat
there on a branch, trembling. He knew
now the Bird Gang had been right. But
Ronnie was even scarier than they'd said.

Suddenly there was a flapping noise, and
some*thing* landed beside him…

Elvis nearly jumped out of his fur.
But it was only the Robin.
"Is everything OK?" she asked.
Elvis shook his head miserably.
"Well, we did try to warn you."
"I know," Elvis groaned. "But I didn"t
listen, just like I didn't listen to Chuck.
This is all my fault! And there's no way
I can save him!"

Then Elvis had an idea. "Wait a minute –
what about you and your friends? I think
I could save Chuck if you helped me."
"*I'd* be happy to," said the Robin. "But
it won't be easy persuading the rest of the
gang. You're not their favourite squirrel,
are you?"

Elvis suddenly felt ashamed of the way
he'd behaved earlier.
"And it will be a tough job even if
we all work together," said the Robin.
"Mind you, we'd love to see Ronnie
taught a lesson. So if you could come
up with a plan…"

Elvis stared at her. A plan to beat Ronnie? It seemed impossible. But unless he could think of one, his best friend was doomed.

"Right," said Elvis through gritted teeth. "Leave it with me."

Then he scampered off into the wood, back towards Ronnie's nest.

Chapter Five

Elvis peeked at Ronnie's nest from the shadows. Chuck hadn't been eaten yet, thank goodness.

But suddenly there was a strange rumbling noise…

"Oh, I beg your pardon," said Ronnie, looming over Chuck. "That was my tummy. I do believe it's trying to tell me it's nearly dinner time…"

Chuck whimpered, and Elvis scowled. "Think," he whispered to himself. "Oh, if only I were clever like Chuck ... what would *he* do if I were in that nest?"

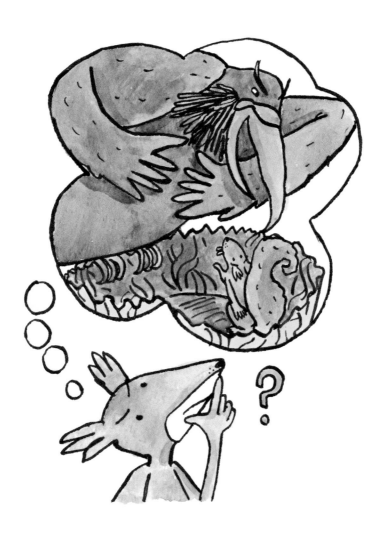

Then Elvis remembered what Chuck had said: *We should check out the area…* Elvis did just that, and immediately saw something interesting. If somebody chewed through that washing line…

…and the branch did *that*…

and Ronnie was standing *there*…

it might just work!

Elvis ran off to find the Bird Gang.
They were on their table.
"Here comes trouble," muttered the
Magpie. "What do you want *now*?"
"Don't be like that," said the Robin.
"Just listen to him, will you?"

"Look, I know I was cheeky to you earlier," said Elvis.
Three birds stared at him stonily.
"But … I need your help to save my friend."

"From Ronnie the Raven?" said the Pigeon. "You must be joking."

"Yeah, how are we supposed to do that?" muttered the Bluetit.

"Actually, I"ve come up with a very cunning plan," said Elvis. "And if it works … well, I promise it will be the funniest thing you've ever seen."

"Ummm … I like the sound of that," murmured the Magpie. "Tell me more…"

Chapter Six

A little later, Elvis and the Bird Gang
were hiding near Ronnie's nest. They
were all feeling nervous, but determined,
at the same time.

"Now remember," said Elvis. "The plan is for me to catch Ronnie's eye and get him to move into the right position. And while I'm doing that, you lot can chew through the washing line. OK, let's go…"

"Hang on a second," said the Magpie, "it ought to be the other way round. You're a squirrel, so you'd be much better at chewing than us."

"And we'd be better at catching Ronnie's eye," said the Pigeon.

"We won't have to get close to him to do it, either," said the Bluetit. "I mean, that might be pretty dangerous. Ronnie can move very fast…"

Elvis was about to say no. He wanted Chuck to see *him* doing the dangerous stuff. Then he noticed the Robin looking at him, and he realised he was making the same old mistake. He wasn't *listening*. "You're right," said Elvis. "That is the best way. Now, places, everybody!"

The Bird Gang took up their positions. Elvis waited a second, then nodded to them … and they swooped down towards Ronnie's nest. They flew around it, screeching and calling him names.

Ronnie hopped onto the side of his nest and hissed at them. He was in just the right place, and Elvis started chewing.

"Clear off, you scruffy vermin," Ronnie screeched, "or I swear I'll…"
But Ronnie never did finish making his threat. Elvis had done a good job, for suddenly…

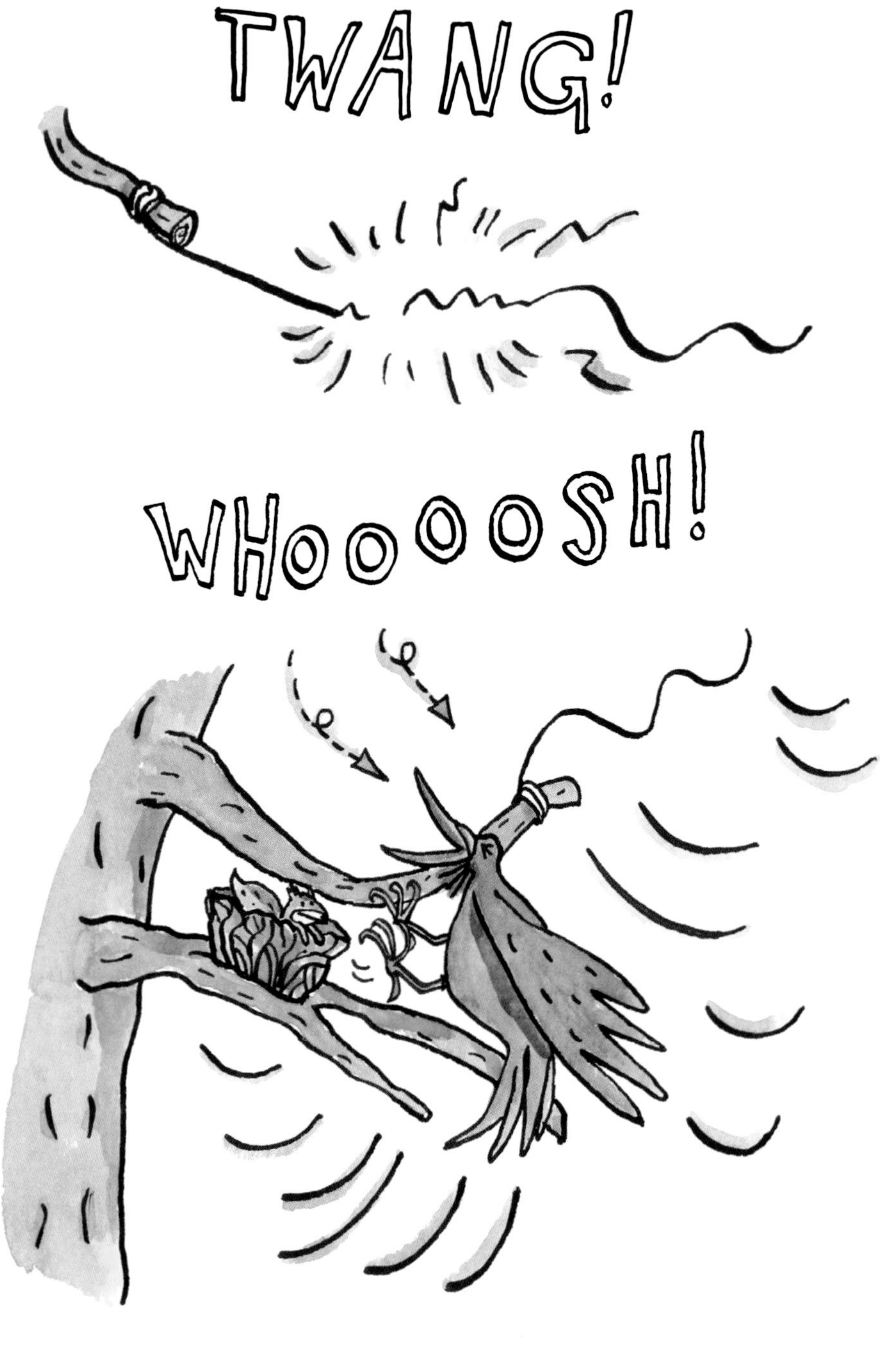
TWANG!
WHOOOOSH!

Ronnie was knocked clean off his perch,
and plunged to the ground.

Elvis and the Bird Gang met on the tree, and everyone laughed … and laughed … and laughed.

Chuck peeped at them over the edge of Ronnie's nest. "Wow, that was so cool!" he murmured. "How did you do it?"

"It was more than just cool," said the Magpie. "It was utterly brilliant!"
The rest of the gang nodded in agreement.

Then the Robin nudged the Magpie.
"Oh, yes…" said the Magpie. "Do you
two fancy joining us for some supper?
There's still plenty of bread left."
Elvis grinned. Now *that* was the best
thing he'd heard all day…